CHELM for the HOLIDAYS

Valerie Estelle Frankel

KAR-BEN
PUBLISHING

KAR-BEN PUBLISHING
A division of Lerner Publishing Group, Inc.
241 First Avenue North
Minneapolis, MN 55401 USA
1-800-4-KARBEN

Website address: www.karben.com

Cover illustration by Sonja Wimmer.

Main body text set in Bembo Std 12.5/17.
Typeface provided by Monotype Typography.

Library of Congress Cataloging-in-Publication Data

Names: Frankel, Valerie Estelle, 1980– author. | Wimmer, Sonja, illustrator.
Title: Chelm for the holidays / by Valerie Estelle Frankel ; [illustrator, Sonja Wimmer].
Description: Minneapolis : Kar-Ben Publishing, [2019] | Summary: Presents ten holiday stories set in the tiny Jewish village of Chelm, where it is said that the angels distributing silliness throughout the world tipped their bowls and spilled it all.
Identifiers: LCCN 2018047733 (print) | LCCN 2018052994 (ebook) | ISBN 9781541560901 (eb pdf) | ISBN 9781541554610 (th : alk. paper) | ISBN 9781541554627 (pb : alk. paper)
Subjects: LCSH: Fasts and feasts—Judaism—Juvenile fiction. | Children's stories, American. | CYAC: Fasts and feasts—Judaism—Fiction. | Jews—Poland—Chelm (Lublin)—Fiction. | Judaism—Customs and practices—Fiction. | Chelm (Lublin, Poland)—Fiction. | Short stories. | Humorous stories.
Classification: LCC PZ7.1.F7514 (ebook) | LCC PZ7.1.F7514 Che 2019 (print) | DDC [Fic]—dc23

LC record available at https://lccn.loc.gov/2018047733

Manufactured in the United States of America
1-45735-42369-12/6/2018

CONTENTS

INTRODUCTION

A long time ago in the Old Country, there was a tiny Jewish village called Chelm. Many people say that when the angels were distributing silliness throughout the world, their bowl tipped, spilling all the silliness into one town—Chelm. They say that the people of Chelm once sentenced a rebellious fish to death . . . by drowning. Did they really milk their horses so the cows wouldn't feel pressured? And when the man who knocked on people's doors to wake them for morning services grew too old to leave his house, did the foolish people of Chelm really pull their doors off the hinges and bring them to him, so he could knock on their doors without the lengthy walk?

The people of Chelm of course celebrated all the Jewish holidays, from Rosh Hashanah through Shavuot, and then round and round again. But on holidays in Chelm, the foolishness always seemed to get in the way . . .

THE HONEYBEES OF CHELM
A Rosh Hashanah Story

Rosh Hashanah was coming, but for some reason, this year there was no honey in the marketplace in the village of Chelm. What would the people of Chelm do? How could they bake their honey cakes? How could they dip their apples in honey?

How will we celebrate Rosh Hashanah without honey? thought Schlemiel. He was the most useless man in the village. He liked to lie on his back and nap all day long, but even he knew something needed to be done about the honey.

Schlemiel had a wife, Mrs. Schlemiel, and a baby, Little Schlemiel. Mrs. Schlemiel was always yelling at Schlemiel for being useless. But now her lip quivered. "No honey for Rosh Hashanah! The baby's first New Year and not a drop of honey."

Schlemiel shuffled his feet. *The New Year was much like the old year*, he mused. The old year had ended with Mrs. Schlemiel yelling at him, and it seemed the New Year was starting the same way.

"I remembered to buy honey in the market last Rosh Hashanah. And I remember what happened. I traipsed all the way to market and back, in the burning sunshine, and I bought a big jar of honey. But the truth is . . ." Schlemiel cleared his throat. ". . . after all that work, I thought a tiny taste wouldn't hurt. So I stuck in my finger and tried just a drop. Then I tried a bit more. And a bit more. It was so good! Then I resolved to stop, and I had a drink of water since the honey was so sticky. But after my drink, all the honey taste was gone. So I had to try just a nibble more. And after that taste— what could you guess?—I needed more water. Well, after a while, all the honey was gone!"

But this year there was no honey to be had in the market. Schlemiel paced the house. Even if there was no honey in the marketplace, surely he could find honey somewhere else. He stopped so suddenly that he tripped over his feet and nearly went sprawling. The pasture south of town!

It was a beautiful meadow, filled with succulent blossoms and, of course, bees. And the bees made honey, didn't they? But how to collect it without being stung?

"I will disguise myself as a flower," Schlemiel decided. "Bees like flowers so much they would never sting one." Schlemiel hurried into the bedroom and pulled the yellow-flowered quilt off the bed. With a flourish, he draped it around himself. The back dragged in the dirt, but from the front, he fancied that he looked quite colorful. A handful of Mrs. Schlemiel's daisies, plucked from the garden and stuffed into his scraggly gray beard, completed his disguise. Thus prepared, he picked up his empty honey jar and scoop and went out.

When the villagers saw him, they mumbled and whispered. What was Schlemiel doing? "Have you gone crazy?" asked Ehud the Baker.

"No. He's bringing flowers to his wife but carrying them in his beard," Grandma Faina cackled.

"I'm hunting for honey," Schlemiel explained. "The bees will think I'm a flower, so they will let me take their honey and will not sting me."

"Dressed like that?" Avram hooted, chewing on an apple. "All you'll get is dirt. Some hunter!"

Children ran behind Schlemiel giggling and shouting. Adults stuck their heads out the windows, attracted by the commotion. By this time, quite a crowd was following Schlemiel as he trooped to the bee pasture. The pasture was beautiful, with autumn flowers blushing pink and orange against the grass. The bees were buzzing in fuzzy yellow spirals.

"Ignore him, bees. He's just a flower," called little Tzipporah. Soon everyone took up the cry. Schlemiel clutched his honey scoop and jar.

Bees zipped around him in confused circles. Who was this giant creature invading their hive? Schlemiel's face burned red and hot from the sun, so much so that the bees couldn't fail to spot it. One of the boldest flew at him, aiming straight for his bulbous, sunburned nose.

With a shriek, Schlemiel swatted the bee away. Too late! His nose bulged to twice its normal size, throbbing with a painful bee sting. Schlemiel turned around and dashed for home with the entire angry swarm of bees behind him.

It was a hilarious sight. Schlemiel raced through the fields, pudgy arms pumping, flushed face sweating, red nose throbbing. His beard blew in his face, nearly masking the swollen nose and covering his eyes. Daisies from his beard scattered in all directions. Mrs. Schlemiel's yellow-flowered bedspread flapped behind him like a bedraggled cape. Following him came the swarm of bees, all intent on puncturing his backside. How he ran! How they flew!

At last, Schlemiel reached his house, flung open the door, and raced inside. He slammed the door before any of the bees could reach him.

Later that day, Schlemiel sat slumped in his favorite chair. His wife continued to wail about the lack of honey.

"Oh, the baby's first Rosh Hashanah. Ruined, ruined!" Her sobs pulsed in time with Schlemiel's aching nose until he was ready to cry himself. And still no honey for the holiday. At last, Mrs. Schlemiel slammed the bedroom door and left him with a cool cloth on his swollen nose.

Suddenly, there was a knock at Schlemiel's door. Very cautiously, he opened it a tiny crack. Bees had never knocked politely on his door before, but there was a first time for everything.

It wasn't the bees. It was his neighbors. Ehud held out a large jar. "It's honey," he said. "And you certainly earned it. L'shana tova."

"Where did you get honey?" Schlemiel protested. "Don't you need it to make your own honey cakes?"

"Oh, it's not our honey, it's yours," Ehud said, beaming. "After you led all the bees away from the hive, we gathered all the honey. This was a great idea, Schlemiel! Maybe next year you can do it again and we'll all have honey for Rosh Hashanah!"

Schlemiel stood there in his tattered bedspread, covered in dirt and sweat. He'd lost one of his shoes in a mud puddle. A few drooping daisies hung from his tangled beard. The bee sting on his nose throbbed achingly. "I may be a schlemiel," he said. "But even I know this is no job for me!"

He thanked his neighbors, took the honey, and shut the door.

Even though Schlemiel refused to be the future bee distracter, the people of Chelm weren't about to discard a good idea. Every year from that day on, one of the villagers donned a colorful quilt and pretended to be a noisy flower until the bees chased him away and the other villagers could collect the honey. Every Rosh Hashanah, Schlemiel could be found hiding under his kitchen table, in an old bathrobe with a protective bucket on his head, awaiting his share of honey.

THE FAST THAT ALMOST DIDN'T END
A Yom Kippur Story

Yom Kippur had nearly come to an end. People had stopped saying, "Have an easy fast," and were beginning to mutter under their breaths, "What's for dinner?"

The elders of Chelm clustered in their council room. "The afternoon break is almost over," Leib the Lackwit murmured. Beside him, Uri the Unwise snored, with his head in his arms.

"Then we'll need to daven the Ne'ilah service to end the fast," said Fishel the Foolish. His belly rumbled loudly. The bellies of the other Elders echoed the sound.

"It'll take another hour to get through all those pages," said one Elder.

"So much time until sundown," said another.

"Maybe we could sleep through it," said a third.

"Or maybe we could end the fast early, right now," Uri the Unwise suggested unwisely.

Farfel the Fat raised his eyebrows. "You mean, we could just say that it's dark enough and have our dinner now? Break the fast early?"

"We're the Elders. We'll simply declare that the holiday is over."

Simon the Simpleminded cleared his throat. "Isn't that the rabbi's job?" They all thought about the devoted rabbi, praying in the synagogue.

Uri the Unwise shrugged. "The rabbi won't mind. He must be hungry too. Let's declare that it is now night and everybody can eat!"

Quick glances to the kitchen convinced the Elders that it was indeed time for Yom Kippur to be over.

The Elders always ate together to break the fast, ever since the time Farfel the Fat ate so much he couldn't pass through his front door. The Elders hadn't noticed he was missing, and they left him out of an entire week's decision-making! When he finally emerged from his house, he was the only one not wearing his hat upside down to catch low-flying ducks.

The Elders went out to check the sundial, but as the villagers had built a roof over it to protect it from the rain, it no longer told time. They couldn't tell whether the fast was over. They went to check the synagogue's skylight—which was always open so that sunlight wouldn't be permanently trapped indoors.

Fishel the Foolish pointed to the ceiling. "Look, it's dark. Clearly, day's already gone."

"I think it's a cloud over the sun," said Leib the Lackwit hesitantly, but nobody paid attention.

"Rivka, the fast is now over," said Gimpel the Great Fool. "Please bring us our dinner."

Rivka climbed the stairs from the kitchen and burst in on the Elders, hands on her hips. The tight little bun at the back of her head made her face look as round as a potato. Normally she wore a huge, flour-covered apron, but today she wore her simplest white dress, the one with the wide belt with embroidered doves.

"Oy," she muttered. She'd been napping after a morning of telling stories to the littlest children. "The fast isn't over until the rabbi declares the holiday completed. You know that."

"Ridiculous! We're the Elders, and we're ready for our supper."

"Yes, where are the boiled eggs and gefilte fish?"

"And the bagels? We must have bagels."

All the Elders roared their approval.

Rivka smiled an odd little smile. "I'm afraid all the food is gone."

"*What!*" they chorused.

"Before Yom Kippur, you were afraid the people of Chelm wouldn't have the willpower to fast all day. Don't you recall the orders you gave?"

Leib the Lackwit shuddered. "We're leaders. You can't expect us to remember our decisions."

"Or care about the consequences," Farfel the Fat chimed in. "Now feed us. We want to eat."

At that point, Uri the Unwise's stomach growled, setting the table to shaking.

"Nu, so what did we order, Rivka?" asked Gimpel the Great Fool, seeking the quickest way to get the food served.

Rivka smiled again, enjoying the moment. "Yesterday evening, when everyone felt completely stuffed, you ordered the people to put all their food into a giant sack. That way, you figured, no one would sneak even a bite before services ended. Then you—"

"I remember, I remember," Itzik the Silly said. He winced. "We hoisted it into the tallest tree, didn't we?"

Gimpel the Great Fool straightened. "Get the ladders and ropes!"

"No, wait, we thought of that," Simon the Simpleminded said. "In fact, we threw all the ladders and ropes into the river. No sense hiding the food where we could reach it."

"Well, since we can't eat now, we'll have to wait." Farfel the Fat blinked back tears. Beside him, Itzik the Silly rubbed his empty stomach.

"And what happens after sundown?" Rivka asked. She was hungry herself, after all. "Will the food magically fall from the sky?"

The Elders exchanged worried glances. "The people will go home, looking for their dinners . . ."

"And they'll see the food's all gone . . ."

Gimpel the Great Fool's head thudded onto the table, barely muffled by his enormous whiskers. "They'll be furious. The year's barely started, and already they won't trust us."

Uri the Unwise nervously began to twist his long beard in knots. "So what do we do? We're the leaders of this town, and the people look to us to solve their problems. Even the ones we created."

They exchanged panicked glances. Then the Elders said in one voice: "Let's ask the rabbi!"

Everyone trooped into the sanctuary.

"Ah, back for Ne'ilah," the rabbi said happily. He was long used to Chelm's foolishness, although he had been born in a town far away.

"Of course," Uri the Unwise said guiltily.

"Yes, yes," the others chorused.

"Although . . ." Gimpel the Great Fool added.

"Yes?" encouraged Farfel the Fat.

"I'm afraid we tied all the town's food up in a tree so people wouldn't be tempted to break the fast early, so after services no one will be able to break the fast," he said.

The rabbi's forehead creased. "Surely a ladder—"

"We threw all the ladders and ropes into the river," Gimpel the Great Fool said in an even faster rush.

Just then, the people of Chelm flooded into the synagogue for the Ne'ilah service. They were hungry, and anxious to break the fast. The rabbi straightened his kittel and his tallis.

"What do we do?" Fishel the Foolish asked in a frantic whisper. "If the people find out there's no food—"

"There's no food?!" a dozen voices exclaimed. The entire village of Chelm now filled the synagogue.

"Of course there's no food," the rabbi said in a

loud voice. "Today is Yom Kippur, and we should be focused on healing our souls and asking forgiveness. At last, we've reached Ne'ilah, the time when the heavenly judgment Hashem inscribes on Rosh Hashanah is finally sealed."

"But after services—?" Itzik the Silly asked in an even more unsteady whisper. "They'll be so hungry, they'll eat *us*. And we're not even kosher."

The rabbi rested a hand on Itzik's shoulder. "All the Elders of Chelm are here, awake from their naps. In fact, they were the first ones through the door for the Ne'ilah service. Now, I consider that a miracle. Let us pray to Hashem to protect the people of Chelm in the coming year." He smoothed his beard.

"They surely need it," he added under his breath. "And then," he added in a louder tone, "perhaps Hashem who loves us and shelters us may produce yet another miracle. If the Elders stay through Ne'ilah, another miracle is not much to expect."

The congregants opened the ark. The rabbi began the Ne'ilah service, with its beautiful melodies and touching psalms. The Elders of Chelm prayed as they never had before. They begged Hashem to forgive them their foolishness (no matter how much more they might commit the following day), and they prayed that Hashem would protect all the people of Chelm and not let them suffer for the Elders' mistakes.

Just outside the synagogue, a heavy sack tied to a very tall tree drooped a tiny bit. High winds pushed the bundle up, twisting the branch that held it. Each time the sack swung up and then down, it drooped lower and lower.

"May we be inscribed in the Book of Life," the rabbi said. He lifted the shofar and blew a long, piercing note: *Tekiah Gedolah*! The people gasped. The walls shook. And overhead, a single branch broke. Down tumbled the sack of food, through the open skylight, to land right in front of the ark!

"Hashem provides," the rabbi murmured as the hungry congregants stared at the sack. He pointed up through the open skylight to the glorious, windy heavens. Night had fallen, with three stars dotting the sky. "Next year in Jerusalem! May Hashem inscribe us all in the Books of Life, Prosperity, and Peace. Now, go and—"

Before the rabbi could say another word, the ravenous people of Chelm tore open the sack. Boiled eggs, gefilte fish, kugel, lox, and dozens of bagels came spilling out. And the people ate until everyone was full, even Farfel the Fat.

THE VERY BEST GUEST
A Sukkot Story

"Wait! Wait!" called Yosef the Butcher.

With difficulty, Farfel the Fat halted his ponderous steps. Folks in Chelm said you could never tell whether Farfel was passing by or if Poland had finally built a railroad past Chelm; the rumbling was much the same. Farfel looked over his shoulder, careful not to lean so far that he'd topple onto his ample behind.

"What is it, Yosef?"

Yosef the Butcher ran up, panting like a carp out of water. "Please, come visit my sukkah tomorrow!"

"Your sukkah?"

"Yes. It's a sort of tent, with cloth walls and a roof of branches so you can see the stars. I'm spending the week in it to thank Hashem for the harvest."

"What! That's just like my sukkah! Did you copy mine?" Farfel's face flushed florid with frenzied fury.

Yosef shook his head quickly. "Oh, no, Farfel. Did you perhaps copy mine? I just wanted to ask if you would be our guest for dinner in the sukkah. My wife's been baking apple kugels all week."

Farfel's eyebrows rose. No matter who had stolen whose idea, apple kugel changed the subject entirely. "Thank you, I'd be pleased to come. But why are you asking me? I thought Frumpel was your best friend."

Yosef's face colored. "That was before he said my sukkah had so many holes in the roof that birds would fly in and eat my supper. Now Frumpel and I are having a contest to see who can invite the more distinguished guest."

"How many holes are there in your sukkah roof?" Farfel asked with some alarm. Battling a flock of birds for the kugel lessened the appeal of the invitation.

"Well, you see, the commandment for building a sukkah orders us to be able to look up through the canopy and see three stars. But my old bubbe is blind. So I kept clearing away branches, hoping she'd be able to see, until there was, well, no roof left."

"Ah," Farfel said. "So you want me to eat in your sukkah with no roof, hoping the birds don't gobble the meal first? No, thank you. Besides, then I won't have any guests of my own. I'm not about to let you invite a better guest than I do." And with that, Farfel wobbled down the road to invite Simon the Simple-minded to his sukkah for dinner.

Simon was prepared to accept the invitation, until he heard there was a contest to invite the best guest. Then he snorted at Farfel's invitation (a little reluctantly, since Farfel always served an enormous supper) and decided to enter the contest himself. He went to invite Leib the Lackwit.

He pounded on Leib's door. "Leib, Leib, you must come to my sukkah for dinner!"

Leib blinked slowly. He had been calculating how many sneezes there were in the world on any particular day, since that seemed a most important thing to know. "What's the matter, Simon? Is your sukkah about to explode?" He thought it out. "If it is, I won't come."

Simon shook his shaggy head. "Oh, no, nothing like that. You see, we're having a contest to invite the best guest. And that's you."

"But then I won't have a guest," Leib protested.

"I can't possibly come. Say, do you think one sneeze per ten people per day is an exaggerated figure?" But Simon had already left.

"I suppose I should join the contest and find my own guest," said Leib. He slowly stood up, since he hated standing if he had any choice in the matter. Leib smiled to himself. "I'll invite Avram, the richest man in this village," he muttered. "He will be the most important guest by far."

In his book-filled study, Avram thought about the invitation. "You want me to come because I'm important?"

"Precisely." Leib was glad Avram had caught on so quickly. It would give him more time to sort sneezes.

"But I'm always the host," said Avram. "My wife will be disappointed if we don't invite guests. She already baked the rugelach. If anyone gets to be sukkah hosts, it should be us."

"Look," Leib suggested. "We can swap. I'll be your guest, and you be mine."

"Will we eat in your sukkah?"

"Well, yes, but my wife and I will be honored to be your guests."

"At your house."

Leib shrugged.

"No," Avram said. "I'm sure I can find someone to eat at *my* house." And he strode off, determined to ask the Chief Elder himself to be his guest.

Gimpel the Great Fool was flattered to be asked but had to decline when he heard a competition was happening. He couldn't be left out of such a contest! Leaving Avram standing at his door, he stopped suddenly in the street. "Who in this town is greater than I, the greatest Elder of all? Whom can I possibly invite to my sukkah?" And he simply stood there, frozen like a statue next to the main square.

In the main square, the students had just finished decorating their own sukkah with paper chains and popcorn strings. Painted gourds and red apples dangled from green and yellow yarn. Holiday cards blanketed each of the wooden walls in a frenzy of color. And over the door hung a page of handwritten blessings.

Gimpel studied an odd pile of flags and banners moving across the floor. Surely, such piles didn't usually walk around on stockinged legs. "Is someone under there?" he asked hesitantly.

"Of course," a girl's voice said. "It's me, Chava."

"Ah. I knew flags could wave by themselves, but walking seemed rather ambitious. What's that you've written in Hebrew?"

"It's an invitation for Hashem to enter the sukkah and celebrate with us," Chava said. "With Hashem should come all the matriarchs and patriarchs who started the Jewish nation. Are you coming too?"

Gimpel raised his eyebrows. "It seems that you children have invited better guests than any of us could dream of. While we were busy squabbling over which of us was the most important, you were the ones to see the truth. Yes, of course I'll celebrate with you. Better yet, each of you run home and tell your fathers and mothers to bring all their holiday foods and join us here. That way, Hashem will be guest to us all, and we can all enjoy Hashem's bounty together."

And so they did.

THE OILIEST MIRACLE
A Hanukkah Story

Every Hanukkah, the people of Chelm lit a giant menorah in the center of town. Everyone would sing in its flickering light and dance around the square in a giant hora. Then the children would collect their Hanukkah gelt and go home to play dreidel until their parents shooed them off to bed. This year, however, there was a problem.

"Where's the oil for the menorah?" Gimpel the Great Fool asked. All the Elders sat around their great table, where they debated puzzles every day. "It ought to be in the synagogue where it always is, but there's no sign of it. The oil jar is empty."

"Tonight is the eighth night," Fishel the Fool-ish said. "We should've had enough oil for all eight nights. Did someone count wrong?"

"Well, the first night, there's one light," Leib the Lackwit said, counting on his fingers. "Then two, then three, then four, then five . . . I'm out of fingers on this hand. Quick, someone pull my shoes off."

"Wait, wait," Simon the Simpleminded protested. "Every night there's also a shamash."

Everyone suddenly realized the mistake. They had forgotten the helper light that kindled the others, and so they had run short of oil.

Gimpel the Great Fool groaned. "Where can we get oil on the eighth night of Hanukkah? Everyone is using the last of their own supply as we speak. There can't be any left for the town menorah."

The Elders had many ideas. "Fill the menorah with water. Perhaps in the dark, it won't know the difference," said one Elder.

"If olives, which are small and oval, produce oil, why not grapes? Let's burn grape juice instead," said another.

"That's silly. Let's pronounce that this is the first day of Hanukkah. We had oil then, so that'll make sure we have oil now."

And so it went.

"Let's ask the people to donate some of their oil,"

Fishel the Foolish said. "My wife and all her sisters and cousins and aunts don't have any left, but someone must."

Hurriedly, they sent Gimpel the Great Fool to beat on every door and borrow as much oil as possible. However, the people had been frying latkes and doughnuts all week. Now they had only a little cold grease shining on the very bottoms of their pans.

"We will have to borrow oil from the Ner Tamid," Uri the Unwise said at last. The Eternal Flame hung above the altar and was always burning. If it always burned, what was the harm in borrowing some oil?

So they hurried over to the Ner Tamid and scooped out most of the oil. Immediately, the flame started to burn low.

"Quick, more oil!" Itzik the Silly shouted. "We can't let the Ner Tamid go out!"

"How about the streetlamps?" called Simon the Simpleminded. In Chelm, a few lamps lined the main street, burning oil each night. But now, reasoned the Elders, oil was more precious than light. So they skimmed most of the oil out of the streetlamps and poured it onto the Ner Tamid.

Then the people of Chelm began complaining. "The street is dark! We can't see our way through the village to reach the menorah in the main square," they said. So what was there to do but pour the oil they had taken from the Ner Tamid into the lamps?

"We could dig for oil," Fishel the Foolish said. "Oil comes from the ground, after all." So the Elders, with their white beards and greatcoats, gathered in front of the meeting hall and began to dig with shovels. Of course, the earth was frozen as hard as stone and cold as an icicle. No matter how hard the Elders shoved their shovels, they couldn't budge the frozen ground. But at last, they managed to dig a small hole. In it, they found dirt. And rocks. And gravel. But there was no oil. At last, exhausted and defeated, they returned to their council room.

Utterly disappointed, the Elders regarded the empty menorah through the frost-covered window. It seemed that on the last, most joyous night of Hanukkah, there would be no celebration.

"The holiday dinner's ready," called Rivka the Cook. "After all that running around and digging, you've surely worked up an appetite." She brought in a huge platter of doughnuts and an even larger mountain of latkes, crisp and brown, on a tray shiny with grease.

"We're too miserable to eat," Gimpel the Great Fool said. "Just forget it."

"Not so fast," said Fishel the Foolish, motioning Rivka away from the platter. "We're hungrily miserable, after all."

"Yes, we should eat *more* in a crisis," Leib the Lackwit suggested, already piling his plate high.

"And we shouldn't waste the doughnuts," mumbled Uri the Unwise, his mouth close to his plate as he shoveled the latkes in.

"Why are you all so miserable?" Rivka asked. "It's the last night of Hanukkah. Soon we'll light the giant menorah in the town square and see it fully lit at last."

"Not without oil," groaned Gimpel the Great Fool. Perhaps eating eight doughnuts in under a minute had been a mistake.

"There's no oil?" asked Rivka.

"No." Gimpel straightened at the thoughtful look on Rivka's face. "Don't tell me you have some!"

"I used up all the oil frying the latkes and doughnuts for dinner. But I have an idea." Rivka collected nine big latkes from the greasy platter, slapping the

Elders' hands away long enough to snatch away the latkes. Outside, in the main square, she placed one latke in each menorah cup. She kindled the shamash latke and used it to light all the other latkes. A delicious smell of frying oil spread through the square. Drawn by the marvelous smell and the golden lights, people hurried to the square. Then, by the light of the burning latkes, the villagers danced and sang far into the night and had a happy holiday after all. The Elders continued with their enormous feast until their bellies ached, every single one.

THE DAY THE BIRDS FLEW DOWN
A Tu B'Shevat Story

Minna was busy planting for Tu B'Shevat, the birthday of the trees. She eyed the potted cherry saplings proudly, fingering a curled leaf. Soon the trees would be ten feet tall.

"Ah, Minna. Busy planting, I see. I broke your ladder this morning. Hope you don't mind."

Minna blinked as her neighbor Velvel's head popped up on the other side of the hedge.

"How did you break my ladder?"

Velvel scratched his head. "It was the strangest thing. I wanted butter without all the work of churning it, and I thought if the cow stood high enough, the falling milk might shake itself into butter. So I borrowed your ladder and tried training my cow to climb it. But can you imagine? She broke through all the rungs and tumbled to the ground."

"Is the cow all right?"

"Yes, and she was shaken enough to give butter on her own!"

Minna eyed the cherry saplings. Without a ladder, she wouldn't be able to pick the topmost cherries. Everyone knew the best cherries grew at the top. She thought for a moment. How would she be able to pick the best cherries? Aha! She decided to plant the saplings upside down, with the branches in the ground and roots sticking up high into the sky. "How clever I am," thought Minna with a satisfied smile. "Now I'll be able to pick the best cherries. There's no need for me to reach the roots."

She glanced over the top of the hedge. There sat Velvel in a garden chair with his eyes closed. "Velvel!" she called. "What are you doing?"

Velvel opened his eyes. "Planting trees, of course."

"What kind?"

"Matzah ball trees!"

Minna scratched her head. "I've never heard of those before."

"Of course not. I'm the first to have the idea.

See, I put a few grains of matzah meal on the ground and next spring I'll have enough matzah balls for a year's worth of Shabbat dinners."

Minna had nearly finished planting her upside-down cherry trees, when she heard a yell. She looked over the fence and had to smile.

"Hey, you! Shoo. Go on, fly away!" called Velvel. As soon as Velvel had closed his eyes on the scattered matzah meal, the sparrows flew down and started gobbling it all up.

Velvel hurled handfuls of matzah meal at the tiny birds, but that only made them happier as they hopped all over his orchard.

"They ate my apple seeds this morning," Minna said.

"They didn't eat my seeds," said her son Aaron, walking through the gate. He was home from school, where he had been digging a new garden with his friends. "Because we were planting nails," he said proudly.

"Nails?"

"If they sprout, we could get a whole house!"

Later that day, other neighbors came by with their complaints. The birds had nibbled everyone's new plantings. Clearly, the best strategy was to plant the seeds somewhere the birds couldn't reach. But where would that be?

Uri the Unwise had planted his corn seeds on his basement floor. "Surely, birds won't get in here," he thought.

Feivel had planted his apple seeds in pots of wet cement. "After the cement hardens, not a single beak will break through," he said. And he was right. All the birds stayed away.

All over Chelm, people piled heavy rocks on their seeds or hid them under floorboards and mattresses. Surely, the birds would leave their new plantings alone now.

A week later, children hurried from house to house to check on the seeds. Not a single one had sprouted, not the matzah ball trees or even the nail bush. Imagine that!

"Now what will we do?" Velvel moaned. "If we plant the seeds in sunlight and dirt, the birds will just gobble them up!"

The children slumped in Minna's empty garden. Their school garden was equally barren, without a single raisin tree or yarmulke vine. "We need the Elders," Aaron muttered. His nail bush hadn't so much as sprouted one metal point, despite all the watering.

"The Elders are baffled," Simon the Simple-minded said. He looked mournfully at the pot that should have held his meshuggah nut tree. It hadn't grown a bit, despite being locked in the closet away from the birds. He had come over to Minna's to borrow some fertilizer.

Little Tzipporah, six and barefoot, giggled. "We should feed the birds other things. Then they won't want our plantings. It's Tu B'Shevat for them, too, you know."

All the villagers stared at one another.

"That's a wonderful idea," said one villager.

"We should make her an Elder," said another.

"Even though she doesn't have a beard?" asked a third.

"Pshaw, she'll grow one later," said a fourth.

"Let's do as she says," said Simon the Simple-minded hastily, before they asked him to step down from being an Elder in exchange for someone who still took afternoon naps. "Everyone, scatter crumbs in the town square. Let's show these birds how the people of Chelm celebrate."

Minna scattered mandelbrot, Peizel scattered pumpernickel, and Moshe scattered muffins. Velvel even gave in and scattered his matzah ball seeds.

From all corners of the sky, birds descended, chirping and squawking. They flapped over the square, gobbling all the offerings until they were too fat to fly. They waddled along the ground, bulging like feather pillows with feet.

But they left the new gardens in peace, so the people of Chelm could get on with their planting. They planted all sorts of seeds: apples and pears, plums and blackberries (and, perhaps, a few yarmulkes). And all the plants started to grow. Well, almost all. The nail bush still refused to grow.

There was a motion to make Tzipporah an Elder, but the people had forgotten that Tzipporah would have to be able to sign her name. The Elders quickly ruled that a handprint in jam was not sufficient, so they ruled unchallenged, while Tzipporah made tasty mud pies for her winged friends.

THE QuEEN ESTHER MiX-UP
A Purim Story

One special spring night, everyone dressed in Purim costumes and came to hear the reading of the Megillah, the story of Purim. Everyone loved the story of how Esther went before King Ahasuerus, begging to save the lives of the Jews in Persia. Through her bravery, she saved her people. Dozens of little girls attending the megillah reading were dressed as Queen Esther. Fishel the Foolish wore a goose costume, with feathers glued all over. Itzik the Silly was a goat. Ehud the Baker dressed as a giant hamentaschen. And Schlemiel had only one wish— to be dressed up as the king.

He took his wife's Shabbat tablecloth—the white one with the blue border—and draped it around his shoulders for a cape. Then he took a pot of geraniums from beside the door, uprooted the flowers, and dumped out the soil. He cracked the pot into two jagged halves to make the perfect (if a bit lopsided) crown. And with his new finery, he paraded into town.

On his way, he saw the little girls of the village all dressed as Queen Esther. After services, Schlemiel dawdled in the center of town. The baby had been cranky all day, and Mrs. Schlemiel would probably yell at him when he got home.

When Schlemiel reached the meeting hall where the Elders made their judgments, the place was deserted. He was unable to resist the tall wooden chair that belonged to the Chief Elder, and he sat down. Once in the chair, he stretched and smiled. After all, why shouldn't he sit in the Chief Elder's chair? He was the king. As he sat on his new throne, Itzik the Silly wandered into the room in his goat costume. He was crawling on four legs, circling in distress.

"I need some advice and a judgment. Where are the Elders?" He had forgotten that he was supposed to be one.

"Elders!" Schlemiel thundered. "Why do you

want Elders when you have a king? Don't you know that I am King Ahasuerus?"

"Very sorry, I'm sure, Your Majesty. Now, if you could just listen to my problem . . ."

"Our problem," said a voice from somewhere around the goat's stomach.

Schlemiel straightened on his throne and gazed down at the goat standing so far below him. "Go ahead."

"Well, a goat has four legs. Everyone knows that. So I asked my wife to help me out and be the two back legs. But she—"

"I don't want to be the hind end of a goat," the goat's stomach interrupted. "I'd much rather be a duck."

Schlemiel considered the matter. "A duck has two legs, doesn't it?"

The goat nodded. "Everyone knows that, Your Majesty."

"Then my royal decree is that you both be ducks. That way you can be equal, as a husband and wife should be." And the husband and wife took off the goat suit and applauded King Ahasuerus's judgment.

After they left to tear apart their feather mattress to make two duck costumes, Schlemiel went to the window. Where were all the other Elders? Across the road, he saw Gimpel the Great Fool dressed as the man in the moon. He was building a very, very long ladder. *He's probably planning to climb back up to the sky*, thought Schlemiel.

Down the street, Simon the Simpleminded was dressed as a chicken, sitting in the chicken coop beside the real birds. He clucked and flapped his wings and scratched around for corn. Leib the Lackwit stood beside him, dressed as a tree. He kept begging people to plant him. Schlemiel smiled. At last, he had his chance to rule all of Chelm. Best not to waste this opportunity. He sank back in the chair and fell into a deep sleep.

Schlemiel awoke to the sound of little girls' voices. Morning had arrived and with it a full day of Purim. Costumes, treats, plays, and carnivals would fill the village until sundown. He turned to see the little troop of Queen Esthers walk into the meeting hall. Some were crying. Others glared and stamped their feet.

"What's the trouble, young ladies?" he asked.

"We can't figure out which one of us is really Queen Esther," Little Tzipporah said. "And we don't know how to decide."

"That's simple," Schlemiel said. "Since I am King

Ahasuerus, and all of you seem to be Queen Esther, we must have a beauty contest."

He sat down on his throne, and all the little girls paraded before him. About halfway through, Schlemiel realized that he would have to marry the winner. Not only were all of these girls far too young for him, but he already had a wife. What should he do? Without a word to the young Queen Esthers, he burst out of his chair and hurried home.

When he reached the house, he flung open the door. Mrs. Schlemiel screamed in surprise and dropped the baby's spoon.

"Come, come, dear. I am King Ahasuerus, and so you must come to the village center with me and be my Queen Esther. You shall sit beside me on my throne and tell me how wise I am."

"Schlemiel, what are you talking about? Why must I come to the center of town; today is a holiday, and I want to rest. Wait a minute, is that my Shabbat tablecloth?"

"Stop fussing. It's Purim. We should celebrate! Now, since I'm the king, you must be my queen." He held his hand out. "Please, won't you come?"

Mrs. Schlemiel smiled, as the Purim spirit filled her. "You truly wish me to be your queen?"

"None but you."

Schlemiel found the flowerpot he had broken, and miracle of miracles, the jagged crack had split the pot perfectly in half, making two crowns, not just one. He placed the smaller crown on the head of his wife and dug into the chest at the foot of their bed until he found her wedding veil. He draped it around her shoulders so that the embroidered hem drifted to her feet. "There, my dear. Now you're truly my Queen Esther."

They walked hand in hand to the meeting house with the sleeping baby. As the Elders all appeared to be otherwise engaged in their various Purim costumes, Schlemiel and Mrs. Schlemiel happily judged the disputes of the people of Chelm for the rest of the day.

At long last, night fell. Now, in Chelm, there was no electricity. When night came, no one could see once they left the main street. All the people stumbled off to their dark little cottages, got into their pajamas, and climbed under the covers. In the morning, the villagers woke up as themselves again, their costumes no more than piles beside their beds. The foolishness of Purim had ended, and it was time to begin a new day.

HOLEY MATZAH
A Passover Story

The people in the village of Chelm worked together to bake the matzah each year. Rivka mixed all the flour with just the proper amount of water. Each father took a large lump of the dough, and each mother rolled it to just the proper thickness. Then the children pushed the spiked wheel over each piece, making neat little rows of holes. Mendel the Baker's Helper popped the matzah into the big oven, where it toasted for exactly eighteen minutes. A warm, wonderful smell filled the room as trays of the flat crackers emerged from the oven.

The people of Chelm always baked on the day before Passover so the matzah would be fresh and crisp for the holiday.

This year, when it was time for the matzah baking to begin, Mendel carried the big bag of flour into the bakery, then stood there staring at it.

Ehud the Baker noticed him standing like a sun-addled bird. "Nu, Mendel, what's wrong?"

Mendel scratched his head. "Well, we use flour to make the crunchy part of the matzah, don't we?"

"Yes."

"And we use water to soften the dough so we can roll it flat."

"Of course."

"So where do the holes come from?"

Ehud the Baker scratched his head. "The holes? They appear when we roll the matzah with the little wheel."

"But that's impossible. Holes can't just come out of nowhere for free. Don't we have to buy them, like flour?" asked Mendel.

"You're right! Please go to the market and buy a big bag of matzah holes, a bag just as big as the sack of flour."

Mendel hurried off to the market. He asked at every farmer's stall. He pestered the peddlers with their imported spices and even the traders with their baskets of household goods. No one had any matzah holes.

He dragged his feet as he returned to the bakery to make his report.

The baker dropped his head into his hands. "This is a catastrophe! How can we make matzah without holes? The entire village depends on us to provide the proper ingredients, and we don't have them. What can we do?"

"I'll ask the Elders," Mendel said. "They can solve any problem."

The Elders scratched their heads and stroked their beards. "This is a catastrophe! We can't bake matzah without holes."

"Could we use bagel holes?" Leib the Lackwit asked.

"Of course not! Too large," the other Elders thundered.

Gimpel the Great Fool cleared his throat. "We've been making matzah in this town for years and years. Surely, somewhere we have a stash of matzah holes."

The Elders looked everywhere. Farfel the Fat checked between the cracks in every bird's nest. Fishel the Foolish looked under doormats and between the wooden floorboards. Leib the Lack-wit climbed on top of the houses to look between the straws in the thatched roofs. Itzik the Silly took a spoon and plunged it into every keyhole. Simon the Simpleminded and Uri the Unwise scoured the insides of puppies' ears, and spaces between chickens' toes. And Gimpel the Great Fool looked everywhere that the other Elders might have missed. But they couldn't find a single matzah hole.

In the last house in the village, a poor little hut built with sticks and straw, Sarah said to her husband, Caleb the Woodcutter, "Husband, what can we do? We don't have any food. How can we hold a Passover seder with no food?"

Caleb squeezed her hand. "I have our seder plans all decided. In a few hours, Passover will start. Then our wealthy neighbor Avram will open his door and say, 'Let all who are hungry come and eat.' And then, my dear, our worries will be over."

A knock sounded on the door, and Caleb hurried to open it. There stood all the Elders, along with Ehud the Baker, Mendel the Baker's Helper, and a dozen other villagers. Caleb quickly stepped back. "Why are you wandering the streets on Erev Passover? Shouldn't you be baking the town's matzah?"

"That's just the problem," Fishel the Foolish said. "We can't bake matzah without matzah holes."

The village's problem struck Caleb deeply. If not even the wise Elders of Chelm could find matzah holes, how could the village celebrate Passover? "Oh no! This is indeed a tragedy for our village. I wish I could help. But in truth, my wife and I are so poor we don't even have enough food for a Passover seder, let alone matzah holes." He held up an empty sack. "You see, we've used our last cup of flour."

Gimpel the Great Fool stared into the empty sack. "Hashem be blessed! Look!"

Sarah scratched her head. "I don't see anything. Our sack is empty!"

"Far from empty. We've searched all day to find matzah holes. And here, you and your husband have an entire sack! Look how empty it is. The holes must be spilling out of this bag, full as it is."

Ehud the Baker lifted it as if the sack held precious crystal wine goblets. "I must buy these holes from you. The sun will set soon, and there's no time to waste. I will pour the holes onto every piece of matzah, before we bake them in the oven." He threw a handful of silver coins into the hands of Caleb and his astonished wife.

"I will go buy flour and wine and bitter herbs," Sarah said to Caleb.

"Oh, but you must be my guests for tonight's seder," Leib the Lackwit proclaimed. "The words of the Haggadah say, 'Let all who are hungry, come and eat.' Besides, you and Caleb have rescued Passover for our whole village."

"No, you must be my guests," Simon the Simpleminded said. "My sister and I would be honored to have you join us."

"I am the Chief Elder," said Gimpel the Great Fool. "Of course you must celebrate Passover with my family."

And as they argued and argued, it was a miracle that the bakers managed to bake enough matzah for the entire village in time for Passover, but somehow Ehud and Mendel managed it. And they all had a very happy Passover, especially Caleb and Sarah, who were heroes, since they had saved Chelm with their precious sack of matzah holes.

IT WILL GET BETTER
A Lag Ba'Omer Story

The people of Chelm spent weeks organizing the perfect Lag Ba'Omer holiday celebration. First, they'd have a huge picnic out in the fields, to remember the Jewish students who hid in forests to read their holy books when the Romans forbade it. The villagers would sing and dance and pick flowers until evening, when they would end the day with an enormous bonfire.

On the morning of Lag Ba'Omer, all the people of Chelm, down to the smallest children, took their picnic lunches and a pile of brightly colored blankets out to the fields. For a time their celebration went happily, with plenty of songs and laughter. Then dark clouds appeared in the sky. A raindrop landed on someone's cheek. Then another and another. Soon the rain was pelting down.

"Shlomo's barn is right over there!" Rivka shouted.

"We can't picnic in my barn," Shlomo bellowed. "My animals are using the barn."

But it was hard to argue with an entire village of cold, wet people. Even as Shlomo complained, everyone herded into the barn. They chased the sheep and cows outside, and spread their blankets on the hard wooden floor.

Now the barn was dusty and filled with straw that scratched under the villagers' tushies, but they opened their picnic baskets and started to eat. Then someone said, "This doesn't seem much like a picnic. We're indoors!" Since no one wanted to go out into the rain that pounded on the roof like a wild animal, Uri the Unwise ordered everyone to open the windows. Immediately, the wind whistled through the building, chilling everyone inside.

"This isn't much fun," said Ehud the Baker.

"It's Lag Ba'Omer," Grandma Faina said. "Let's just keep celebrating. It will get better."

"Picnics need the sun to be shining overhead," Little Dov said. "Let's open the roof."

As Shlomo loudly voiced his objections, Leib the Lackwit and Itzik the Silly tugged two boards out of the roof. Everyone sat back down to enjoy the picnic. But now, along with the wind, freezing raindrops tumbled into the room. The winds spattered the rain about, ensuring that everyone was soaked and miserable.

"I want to go home," Little Dov moaned.

"It's Lag Ba'Omer," Grandma Faina said. "Let's just keep celebrating. It will get better."

Then the animals started banging at the door. The barn was their home, after all, and they weren't used to the wet and cold. "Let them in," Shlomo said.

So they let the animals into the barn. Before, it had been freezing and wet, with damp prickly straw scattered all around. Now livestock mooed and baaed, smelling as only wet animals can smell. They greedily helped themselves to the picnics, as the villagers inched away.

"This is ridiculous," Schlemiel said.

"It's Lag Ba'Omer," Grandma Faina said. "Let's just keep celebrating. It will get better."

Since it was so cold, the villagers agreed that the best course of action would be to light the traditional bonfire.

Farfel the Fat and Fishel the Foolish piled sticks in the middle of the barn and started a small blaze. The people huddled close, grateful for the warmth. Unfortunately, the fire spread surprisingly quickly, roaring along the floor, devouring straw. Leaping flames closed in on the villagers from all directions.

"Ai! Ai! Ai!" Everyone screamed and ran in a panic. The animals howled and ran in circles, trampling all in their path. Children climbed up into the loft, ignoring the fire as it followed them up the ladder. This could have been a very tragic story, if it hadn't been for the rain pouring through the roof. It quickly doused the fire, making everyone sigh huge sighs of relief.

Shlomo's face boiled bright red. "Look at these horrible burns on my barn. It will take forever to rebuild. And my poor animals, look how frightened they are. Two of the cows have run off, and the rest are mooing as if they're about to be slaughtered."

"It's Lag Ba'Omer," Grandma Faina said. "Let's just keep celebrating. It will get better."

But most of the adults were finished celebrating. A few of the boys pulled out bows and arrows and offered to start the archery tournament.

Although most people agreed that this had already been the most dangerous Lag Ba'Omer ever, even without bows and arrows, the tournament began.

Minna pulled out a few chunks of soap that she had brought to wash the jam from her children's faces. "These will just make white marks when they hit the wall. That won't hurt anyone. It might even clean up this dirty barn."

The archery tournament began, each boy or girl shooting arrows, tipped with soft white soap, at the walls. The spent arrows tumbled to the ground. Soon the children began to slip and slide on the soapy floor. The littlest ones giggled and skated along the floor, twisting and twirling. Then the older children dropped their bows and arrows to slide. Soon all the adults were trying it too. The rain trickled to a stop, and a few glimmers of sunlight shone through the holes in the roof. The people of Chelm paid no attention; they were having too much fun.

Thereafter, every year on Lag Ba'Omer, all the people of Chelm trooped to Shlomo's barn. In wind, rain, or sun, they soaped the floor and slid around in glorious circles. And every year they would pause for a moment, just to allow Grandma Faina to say, "You see? It got better." And she was right. For what other village could boast its own skating rink for the summer holiday of Lag Ba'Omer?

ELIJAH BRINGS THE BLINTZES
A Shavuot Story

Shavuot, the holiday celebrating the receiving of the Ten Commandments, had arrived. The wealthier villagers would stuff themselves with traditional blintzes and cheesecake and cream. But poor Caleb the Woodcutter had none of those things and had never tasted even a blintz. Instead, he went to his neighbor, Avram, to borrow a book to read for the holiday.

When he knocked on Avram's door, he smelled a marvelous aroma drifting from the kitchen.

"What's that smell?" he asked his friend.

Avram motioned for Caleb to enter. "Those are blintzes, to celebrate Shavuot, of course."

"Truly, the Lord's world is full of wonders."

Caleb asked to borrow a book, and Avram quickly agreed. As Caleb stood there, breathing in the warm intoxicating smells, he decided that, just once, he had to try a blintz. He rushed back to his cottage, errand forgotten.

"Wife, I want you to make me some blintzes for Shavuot," Caleb said.

Sarah stared at him. "Husband, we are too poor. We can't afford the ingredients."

"Like what?" asked Caleb.

"Well, the sour cream to go on top, for instance," said Sarah.

"Well, skip the sour cream, then," said Caleb.

"What about cinnamon? Cinnamon costs much too much," said Sarah.

"All right. No cinnamon," said Caleb.

"And the cheese for the filling?" asked Sarah.

"We can use something else, can't we?" asked Caleb.

"Maybe I can come up with something," Sarah muttered as she headed toward the kitchen.

An hour later, she brought a plate of pancakes to the table. Each one was wrapped around a dribble of sour milk. "Here are your blintzes. I hope you like them."

Caleb tried one. "They aren't very good, are they? I mean, I thought they'd taste sweet. The ones at Avram's house smelled like a bowl of honey, but spicier and richer."

His wife huffed, resenting the insult to her cooking. "It's because you've been sitting around the house all day. Go take a walk, breathe some fresh air. Then you'll like them better."

"All right, I'll go. But you should come too."

"Fine, just let me lock the windows."

Everyone in Chelm knew that burglars always climbed in and out of windows to do their evil deeds. Therefore, while the door could be left swinging open, the windows always had to be shuttered and locked.

Only a few minutes after they departed on their walk, Avram came to the door. "Caleb, you forgot your book. See, I brought it for you." He stepped inside the open door and looked around. No one was there. On the table lay a stack of pancakes on a plate. "Well look at that. Pancakes! Pancakes just like my mother made them, when I was growing up. What a pity I can't convince my wife to make these for me. She wants everything covered in sugar and cream. Well, Caleb is my close friend. He won't mind if I have just a bite."

Avram sat down and began to eat. Before he knew it, he had finished the entire platter. "What have I done? My friend is poor, and these pancakes must have been his entire dinner. And now I've eaten it! Wait, I know what I'll do. My wife made lovely blintzes for Shavuot. I'll bring them over here and leave them for Caleb and his wife. I'm sure they'll enjoy them." And so Avram hurried off and did exactly that.

When Caleb and his wife returned from their walk, Caleb sat down at the table and began to eat. He tried a bite and then looked up. "Sarah! You must taste these. They're incredible." So she tasted the blintzes, and immediately both of them stuffed them in their mouths as fast as they could.

The neighbors came by to see what smelled so good. Caleb and his wife explained their miracle recipe to them. "It's blintzes," they said. "Real Shavuot blintzes. And the recipe is so simple. You make a pancake rolled around a little sour milk. Then you go off for a walk, and when you return—blintzes!"

The neighbors hurried home to try the recipe. To their disappointment, their attempts just created simple pancakes, rather than the marvelous blintzes they had smelled.

Caleb listened to their complaints, stroking his short beard and considering the matter very carefully. "Well, if we didn't make these blintzes, who did?"

His wife tugged at his sleeve. "Perhaps it was the prophet Elijah! He does good deeds for righteous people, after all."

Caleb's eyebrows shot up. "What? Why would the prophet Elijah bring us blintzes?"

"We do good deeds, and every Passover we leave out a glass of wine for him. Perhaps he's repaying us."

Caleb considered his wife's words. "You know, perhaps you're right. We've always been good people, and Elijah always comes and drinks our wine. Perhaps this year he's brought us something in return."

"It isn't fair that Elijah brought you delicious blintzes," said Ehud. "We, too, give him wine every Passover, just as you do."

"Well, it must be because I am a worthier man," Caleb said proudly. "The Lord has seen that and chooses to reward me with blintzes. In fact," he said, strutting a bit, "I wouldn't be surprised if he had the angels cook them for me."

"If Caleb's house is such a holy place that Elijah brings blintzes there," said Rachel, "maybe we should tear it down and put pieces of that house in our homes. That way we can share in the holiness."

"It's not the house that's holy, it's the man," Chaya responded. "We must show the Lord that we honor Caleb."

"And how shall we do that? Elect him to the Council of Elders?"

Chaya nodded vigorously. "That's a good idea."

Now Caleb began to tremble with nervousness, because he knew that his thin, scraggly beard wasn't long or thick enough for him to be on the council. The Elders were elected because their splendid beards made them the wisest in the town. But as all of his neighbors stood there praising him, and saying how holy he must be to have Elijah himself delivering his blintzes, Caleb began to swagger around the house. And why shouldn't he be one of the Elders? He might not be as wise as they were, or have as long a beard, but he was a holy man and a good man. He would make a fine addition to the council.

But the other Elders were not so sure. They raised their eyebrows at the crowd clamoring on the council steps. Itzik the Silly shook his head. "We've been Elders for years, ever since our beards grew long enough. How can Caleb be one of us, with that scraggly little tuft?"

Gimpel the Great Fool stroked his beard. "Remind me, why does everybody think Caleb is all of a sudden a holy man?"

"Because the people want blintzes," said Farfel the Fat.

"Then there's no need to make Caleb an Elder. All we need to do is make a rule that anyone who can afford to have blintzes on Shavuot must share them with someone who can't. Then all the people will have blintzes."

The other Elders applauded this wisdom.

That evening everyone gathered in the square. The wealthier men and women of Chelm brought gigantic platters of blintzes, enough for everyone to share. People ate until they were full of cream and sugar and cinnamon. They all agreed it was the best Shavuot ever. And Caleb went back to his cottage and his happy wife. Both had finally eaten all the blintzes that they could hold. Caleb didn't even regret not being chosen as an Elder. Well, maybe just a little.

THE DISAPPEARING CHALLAH
A Shabbat Story

Once a week, on Shabbat, the people of Chelm sleep late. Dawn finds a market empty of aproned people and vegetable carts. Instead, everyone dresses in his or her very best clothes. For the men, this means a dark coat and a broad hat. For the women, this means patterned dresses. Mendel, who cut all his coats in half to save on laundry costs, wears half a jacket. Grandma Faina wears mittens on her feet and shoes on her hands so they'll all get worn out equally (because mittens are cheaper than shoes). And Rivka fills her pockets with cookies to give to the quietest children after services. All the people gather at the synagogue to praise Hashem and to request that their lives be good throughout the year. And then everyone goes off happily, ready for an enormous Kiddush lunch with the rabbi. Well . . . almost everyone.

Lyzer was a very wealthy man. In fact, the people called him Lyzer the Miser, because he couldn't bear parting with a single copper coin.

One morning, Lyzer was snoring his way through services. Farfel elbowed him, and Lyzer shifted a little. Maybe he wasn't paying much attention to the service, but at least he'd shown up, hadn't he? That should be good enough for Hashem. A mild twist of guilt rumbled in his stomach, though it might have been indigestion. He had eaten an enormous Shabbat dinner at the home of Gimpel the Great Fool the previous night, with brisket, herring, gefilte fish, chopped liver, baked apples, and any number of other good things. After all that, he preferred a nap to the rabbi's sermon this morning.

"Long ago, all twelve tribes of Israel lived in Eretz Yisrael, the Land of Milk and Honey," said the rabbi. "And one day Hashem will bring us back. But in return, we must do something for Hashem. We must perform deeds of lovingkindness."

As the rabbi described the deeds—feeding the hungry, clothing the needy, visiting the sick—Lyzer drifted off again. And in his sleepy mind, his thoughts went something like this: "So we need to give something in order to reach Eretz Yisrael? Hashem is a better businessman than I thought. Not that I need milk and honey, especially; I have pitchers of both. In fact, this morning I had milk and honey for breakfast, but I had something else with them: challah! Hmm. If Hashem has an abundance of milk and honey, I can't think of anything nicer to give him than a big loaf of challah. That will definitely get me to Eretz Yisrael."

"Twelve tribes, each caring for the others . . ." the rabbi continued.

"Very well," Lyzer muttered aloud. "Twelve loaves of challah, then. That's fair."

From up in the balcony, Rivka threw a cookie at his head.

The next week, before Friday night services began, Lyzer snuck into the synagogue with a dozen fresh loaves in a drawstring bag. Not knowing what else to do, he placed them inside the ark. He rocked back and forth on his toes for a moment but wasn't sure what to say. Lyzer cleared his throat. "Hello. Here's something for You and all the angels. You see, I want to go to Eretz Yisrael, land of Milk and

Honey. Sorry I fell asleep last week; I really didn't mean it. Just too much herring—you know how that is. I don't suppose you could liven things up this week with a thunderstorm or something? Maybe not. Well, good eating." And Lyzer left.

On the other side of town, Baruch paced the floor. He and his wife, Chaya, had eaten their last scrap of challah that morning. Nothing remained for Shabbat dinner. "Well, wife, what shall we do?" asked Baruch.

"Go to the synagogue. Perhaps the rabbi can do something to help us," Chaya said, twisting her patched kerchief in her hands.

"I can't ask for charity, Chaya!"

"Asking the rabbi to help us is like asking Hashem," Chaya retorted. "Go and see."

So Baruch went to the synagogue. The rabbi was out, so Baruch sat in one of the pews before the ark. In the quiet room, he felt as if he knelt before Hashem's throne. "We are ever in your hands, Hashem," he prayed. "My wife and I have been faithful all our lives, but now we have nothing, only a tattered roof over our heads. Soon we shall starve. I can't ask anyone else for help. I just can't. Surely, in your mercy . . ." Overcome by despair, Baruch stood and opened the doors to the ark. And what did he find there? A bag containing a dozen loaves of challah. "Blessings upon you, Lord. In your goodness you have saved us!" he cried. He snatched the bag and hurried home to his wife.

When Shabbat was over, after the Havdalah prayers, Lyzer opened the ark. Behold, a miracle had occurred! The loaves had vanished. "Amazing!" he said. "Hashem, I see you liked my bread. Look, you barely even left crumbs. Next week, I'll bring you a dozen more loaves—with raisins!" And he did.

Seven days later, Baruch hesitated before the ark. "Lord, last week was a beautiful miracle," he said. "We ate seven loaves and donated two to charity. Then we sold the last three before they went stale. Would you consider blessing us again? Chaya and I—we could really use the help." Though Baruch never would have asked a living person to help him, he didn't feel so embarrassed asking Hashem. It felt good to share his problems, knowing someone was listening. Imagine Baruch's amazement and gratitude when he opened the ark and found twelve more loaves—with raisins!

Every Shabbat for ten years, this giving and taking lasted, with neither party the wiser.

One Friday afternoon, the rabbi forgot his tallis at the synagogue and had to return for it. He walked in just in time to see Lyzer place a cotton bag inside the ark. As the rabbi watched, Lyzer hesitated before the ark, digging a shoe into the dirt floor. "Lord, my wife has arthritis. Her hands cramp, and she can't knead the bread the way she used to. Maybe . . . maybe you could help? Better hands for her mean better bread for you, you know. And please, bring healing to all who suffer and guide us all to Eretz Yisrael. Though there's no rush. I mean, I just bought a new barn." He bowed before the ark and turned to leave.

In his weekly visits, Lyzer had become more and more uncomfortable just standing before the ark, asking to get into Eretz Yisrael, so he started asking Hashem to bless the people of Chelm. This quiet moment before the ark meant a great deal to Lyzer, truth be told, since he had finally found a way to connect with Hashem.

"What are you doing?" the rabbi asked when Lyzer had finished his prayer.

"I'm giving Hashem his bread, Rabbi," Lyzer explained. Of course, after that, he had to tell the rabbi the whole story.

"And you say the challah vanishes every week?" the rabbi asked.

"Of course. Hashem eats it with milk and honey. Very neat, I must say. Never leaves any crumbs."

The rabbi shook his head. "That can't be, but I think . . . well . . . perhaps we'd best just watch for a while."

They hid themselves behind the pews. After a time, Baruch tiptoed into the synagogue and hesitated in front of the ark. "Lord, I probably shouldn't say anything, I mean, I wouldn't even call it a problem, truly. Well . . . the bread's been a bit . . . er . . . lumpy lately. Maybe the angels are careless? Not that I'm complaining, mind you. You know this blessing has saved us over and over. But those angels aren't ready for bakers' awards, believe me." With a brief prayer for the people of Chelm, he took the bread out of the ark.

"What are you doing with Hashem's bread?" Lyzer blustered, leaping to his feet.

"Hashem gave it to me," Baruch replied, startled. "It comes every week."

"But I've been giving this challah to Hashem!" Lyzer said.

"And I've been getting it from Hashem," answered Baruch.

He hadn't known it was Lyzer all along. Baruch would never have asked the stingiest man in Chelm for a gift. But here Lyzer had helped him and his wife, over and over again. Baruch stammered his thanks.

Lyzer mumbled a quick "Don't mention it." Ten years! Worse yet, not a single crumb of the challah had made its way to Hashem. What was Lyzer to do? He hurried over to the rabbi. "Rabbi, Hashem never received my gift!"

"Hashem received it every single week. Don't you think the Lord wants you to help those in need?"

"But how will I get to Eretz Yisrael if I've never given selflessly?" Lyzer asked. "That's why I offered challah to Hashem. I wanted Hashem to see I'm a good person. I may snore during services, but at least I've been giving Hashem a fine gift every week."

"You've done better than that. You have helped a fellow human being," the rabbi said. "Hashem has certainly appreciated your deeds of lovingkindness."

About the Author

Valerie Estelle Frankel is the author of over sixty books. She has taught children of all ages, and currently teaches at Mission College and San Jose City College. She enjoys dancing, acting, and creating costumes. She lives in California.